**Other books in the
Shooting Star series:**

The Big Race!

Sylvia McNicoll

Illustrations by
Susan Gardos

Scholastic Canada Ltd.

For Dad.

Special thanks to Mrs. Fallis, Mrs. Rusin and Mrs. McCammon's grade three classes at Bruce T. Lindley School for their input, especially their drawings.

The author would like to assure everyone that no snails were harmed in any way during research for this book.

Canadian Cataloguing in Publication Data

McNicoll, Sylvia, 1954-
    The big race

(Shooting Star)
ISBN 0-590-24908-8

I. Title. II. Series.

PS8575.N53B54 1996   jC813'.54C95-932865-3
PZ7.M35Bi 1996

6 5 4 3 2 1   Printed in Canada   6 7 8 9/9

Contents

Chapter 1

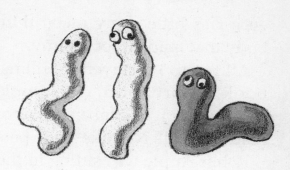

Worm Time

Ten more minutes till home time. Mrs. Leduc just *had* to hand them out soon. They lay curled up on her desk. Three fat worms. I knew which one I wanted.

The pink one had these great black and white googly eyes. But pink is a Barbie-doll colour.

The green worm's eyes were plain black buttons. Kind of like the ones on a sweater. Boring.

The brown one was perfect. It had googly

eyes *plus* little shiny metal things all over its body that made it look slimy.

All recess I'd stayed in, filling out my tenth book report form. Ten books to get one bookworm! It had taken me since September to read them all. Not like some people I know.

Robin Apple was sitting in the seat ahead of me, her light brown hair just begging me to colour it with my markers. In her hands was a book report. Probably her hundredth. I'd heard her and Jenny Sommers tell Mrs. Leduc they'd both read enough for another bookworm. I hoped neither of them would pick the brown slimy one.

"Grade three, next week we will start a new project," Mrs. Leduc told us.

"Nnnnnn," my best friend Marc growled, rubbing at his new buzz cut. Marc's face is round and I like the way his head kind of looks like a bowling ball now.

I really wanted to get a buzz too, but my nose and chin are long, almost pointy. Mom figured I'd look too much like a fuzzy bullet. I pulled at my own hair and growled with Marc. Neither of us likes projects.

I looked out the window. Come on, come on, Mrs. Leduc, the worms.

In the field behind the school, a man was throwing a Frisbee for a big brown dog. The dog's tongue hung out and its ears flew back as it chased after the Frisbee. Dogs are so neat. My only pet is a goldfish.

"Please bring in a large plastic pop bottle," Mrs. Leduc was saying.

We never have pop at our house. I'd have to ask Marc to bring a bottle for me.

Outside, the dog jumped up and snapped the Frisbee out of mid-air. Awesome.

"Also bring your baseball mitts. Next week we begin playing baseball in gym class."

I looked away from the window to cheer with Marc. "Yah, Yah!" We slapped our hands together in high fives. I love baseball.

One of Mrs. Leduc's eyebrows stretched up tippy-toe to touch her hair. "Settle down, boys," she told us. "Where was I?"

"Could we have our bookworms, Mrs. Leduc?" I blurted.

"Neil!" Now Mrs. Leduc's second eyebrow tippy-toed. "In grade three, we raise our hands."

The bell rang then. Everyone started collecting their stuff to go home. Robin's hand shot up.

"Yes, Robin?"

"Mrs. Leduc, my dad is waiting for me outside." She pointed to the man with the dog.

It figured. That dog would have to belong to Robin.

She kept talking. "Could I have my bookworm now so I can leave?"

"Certainly. Neil, Jenny, come choose your bookworms, too. I have just enough for you three today."

I grabbed my book report and tore off to be the first in line. Rats! Robin and Jenny beat me to it.

Don't pick the brown one, don't pick the brown one, I thought.

Robin's hand reached for the slimy-looking bookworm.

"Why don't you take the pink one?" I suggested politely. "It would go great with your Barbies."

"I hate Barbies." She grabbed the brown worm. I groaned.

Robin smiled at me but her blue eyes glared like weapons, lasers maybe. "Why don't you take the green one?" she said. "It would go great with your Ninja Turtles."

Jenny stuck her tongue out at me and chose the pink worm.

That left the green one. The one that looked like someone's nubbly old sweater. I shoved it in my pocket and headed for the door.

Jenny and Robin rushed outside ahead of me, straight over to the dog. The dog smiled big with all its teeth.

My goldfish, Fido, just opens and closes his mouth. You can't ever tell if he's happy. And his eyes are like the buttons on the bookworms.

The dog jumped all over Robin and licked her

face. Then it rolled on its back and Jenny patted its tummy. Robin's dad leaned down and snapped on a leash. He held the loopy end out to his daughter.

But Robin smiled at Jenny instead. She said, "You can walk Prince if you like."

Jenny took the leash and smiled back as the dog stood up.

Prince's fur looked so shiny, I wanted to run up and pat him, too. And to walk him, whoa! That would be great. The only thing I get to do with Fido is shake out fish food.

"You can walk Prince if you like," Marc repeated in a high sissy voice. "Ecch!" He stuck his finger down his throat. "Never mind, Neil," he went on. "Baseball in gym next week." He punched me in the shoulder. "We'll be able to show those girls a thing or two."

"Yeah," I agreed.

So what if Robin could read faster than me and owned the slimy bookworm I wanted? So what if she had a dog that caught Frisbees? *I'm* the best at baseball. Robin would see that on Monday.

Chapter 2

Rotten Apple

Monday, it rained all day.

Tuesday, the rain started at noon.

Wednesday, purple clouds covered the sky in the morning but I packed my glove just in case. And I got lucky.

That afternoon, Mrs. Leduc squinted at the dark sky outside our classroom window. "Since there's a book fair in the gym, we'll chance going outside."

"Whoo hooo!" Marc cheered with me. He

stood up, lifted and dropped his arms. Then I got up and did the same thing. Craig was about to continue the wave but Mrs. Leduc caught him by the arm.

"Boys," Mrs. Leduc warned, one eyebrow starting to stretch, "shall we stay inside and do line dancing instead?"

"No, Mrs. Leduc." Craig slumped back in his seat.

Then Mrs. Leduc assigned teams. After she was finished, Robin Apple waved her hand in the air.

Mrs. Leduc called on her. "Yes, Robin?"

"Can I get the baseball equipment?"

Mrs. Leduc smiled. "Certainly. Team number one, follow Robin out."

Marc looked at me, squeezed his neck with his hands and pretended to choke. He'd been put on team one.

Robin stuck her tongue out at him as she stood up.

"Team two will follow Jenny Sommers in a few minutes," Mrs. Leduc said.

My turn to squeeze my neck. I was a two.

From my seat, I watched Robin Apple and her team march out the door. She was wearing brand new sneakers with red lights in the back that flashed on and off.

When my team finally made it to the field, Robin cartwheeled across the baseball diamond while her friends cheered. I wanted her to trip and fall flat on her face. But she didn't. "Show-off," I muttered to Marc.

"That Robin Apple!" Marc grumbled.

"Rotten apple?" I repeated loudly, not hearing him clearly.

All the kids snickered.

"Yeah! Rotten Apple, that's it," Marc yelled. "Robin's the teacher's wormy rotten apple."

I laughed along with him.

With her hands on her hips, Robin stared at me, her eyes like lasers. I made myself laugh harder.

"Can we bat first?" Jenny Sommers asked when Mrs. Leduc caught up to us.

"We'll go by the class list," Mrs. Leduc

answered. "Line up in order, alphabetically."

That meant Robin batted first. Of course.

"Neil, you can play centre field," Mrs. Leduc called. "Marc, go line up with the others."

I cupped my hand around my mouth and shouted to the other outfielders, "We better stay in close. Girls can't hit that far."

Robin set her lasers on kill. She picked up the bat and swung it a few times. "Ready," she called out.

Jenny Sommers pitched a soft lob.

Robin smashed the ball. It spun hard and fast in my direction.

"Go for it, Neil," Marc yelled at me. He should have been cheering for his own team.

The ball whizzed past my ear and bounced behind me. I chased it, snapped it up and threw it over to Jenny. Robin was already closing in on second base.

Jenny dropped the ball and Robin kept running. Second base, third base — the red lights on her sneakers flashed all the way to home.

Chapter 3

Pop Fly

"**Y**ay, Robin!" all the kids on her team shouted.

All except Marc, that is.

Robin grinned and did a couple of front flips.

"Aw, Jenny! Why couldn't you catch the ball?" I yelled.

"Why couldn't *you*?" she yelled back. "It went right past your head, you moron."

Mrs. Leduc's eyebrow stood on its tippy-toe again. "No name calling, Jenny," she told her.

"Neil, we all make mistakes." She faced the others. "Batter up, please."

Robin's team took forever to strike out. Finally, it was our team's turn at bat. My last name is Boisvert so I stepped up to the plate first.

A drop of rain landed on my nose. "Hurry up and pitch, Robin!"

Robin pushed her hair behind her ears, shifted her Expos hat around backwards and wiped her hands on her baggy shorts. Then she locked her lasers on my forehead. Taking her time, she carefully wound up.

A second raindrop hit my nose. "Come on, come on!" I called. The ball suddenly shot past me.

"Strike one," yelled Jenny.

Raindrops were sprinkling steadily on my face now. Robin wound up even more carefully.

I swung too early this time.

"Strike two."

"Nobody made you umpire, Jenny!"

"Last pitch, Neil." Jenny grinned.

"Shut up!"

Both Mrs. Leduc's eyebrows nearly jumped off her head. "Play ball, Neil," she said quietly.

The sprinkle turned into a shower. This was my last chance. Any moment now, Mrs. Leduc would make us go in. I trained my eye on the ball, the way Mom always told me I should.

Robin set her eyes on kill and pitched.

The ball made a beeline for my bat. If I hit it now, no one would mind that I'd missed the last two pitches. If I hit it now, I'd run like fire, score a homer and start my team winning. If I hit it now, the rest of the season would be great. I knew it.

I waited till the perfect moment. When I swung, every muscle in my body put power behind that bat.

Tok! I love the sound a bat makes when it slams into a softball. It's hollow and hard and makes me feel powerful. My ball headed straight up, so high I thought it would crack the sky open. It was a homer for sure. I burned across the field.

"Lean and mean, Neil's the running machine," Marc cheered.

And I was — skinny and fast.

The sun, peeking out from between the clouds as I headed towards second base, blinded me. Where was the ball? The whole class stared up. This was amazing. I had to stop and watch, my tongue out to catch some raindrops.

The ball headed down. Robin backpedalled from the pitcher's mound in slow motion, never lowering her eyes from the sky. She couldn't, could she? She wouldn't, would she? She held her glove high and we all waited.

Chapter 4

Project Slime

*C*lup! It was the muffled sound a softball makes when it's trapped by a glove.

"Great catch, Robin!" Mrs. Leduc cheered.

I was still staring at the sky, not wanting to believe what had happened. Rain washed over my face as though the ball had flown so high it had cracked open a cloud.

Robin stood there, ball in glove, a big smile on her face.

"Let's go in now, class. It's raining too hard."

I stayed rooted to the spot. "Aw, Mrs. Leduc. It's stopping, I can tell. Can't we play some more?"

Mrs. Leduc dashed under the roof of the school. "Another day, Neil," she shouted back to me. "Come in, you're getting soaked."

Back inside the school, Mrs. Leduc said, "Does everyone have a plastic pop bottle for that project I told you about last week?"

"Marc, you remembered, didn't you?" I asked, turning in my seat. His red face told me he hadn't. "Aw, great! You promised."

"I had them all set. Two bottles right near my cereal bowl. Honest, Neil."

"For those of you who forgot, don't worry. Team up with a partner and share. Marc, Neil, go with Robin."

Robin leaned away from us, covering her bottle with her arms. Marc stuck a finger down his throat and pretended to gag.

"Do we have to?" I asked Mrs. Leduc.

"Raise your hand if you want to ask something, Neil."

My arm shot up.

Mrs. Leduc shut her eyes tightly. "Yes, Neil, your snail will have to share a home with Robin's."

"Snail!" I called out. "Is that our project?"

Mrs. Leduc nodded, smiling.

"Cool," Marc said. "I thought we were going to have to grow some dumb plant."

Both Mrs. Leduc's eyebrows reached for her hair. "I'm going to come around now with some lettuce for you to plant." She looked at Marc when she said that. "Make sure you have your bottles ready. The instructions are on the board."

Following the line where the label had ended, Robin carefully cut the top off the plastic bottle. Marc laid down the rocks. I put a layer of black earth on top. Mrs. Leduc handed us each a small lettuce leaf with roots.

"The lettuce will make the bottles homey for them. Your snails will still need fresh grass and leaves every day. Now, when you're ready, I'll give each of you your new pet."

Robin, Marc and I shot up our hands. Mrs.

Leduc handed us each a snail. Mine was a speckled woody colour. His shell twisted around like a cinnamon bun. Two joysticks — Mrs. Leduc called them antennae — poked out of his little wormy head.

"Think of a name you like," Mrs. Leduc said and walked to Jenny's desk.

"Gross! My snail slimed me," Zachary called.

"Huh, huh," Marc laughed evilly. "Project Slime. I love it."

"Mine looks like Elvis," Jenny announced proudly. "See how his lip curls around?"

"That's his shell," Joshua told her.

"No — there! Look! See his little lip curl?"

"I want to call my snail Elvis," Jennifer Mistry said.

"Me, too," Jennifer Dopko called out.

"That's okay. Why don't we put all three snails together in my bottle?" Jenny suggested. "Yours can be Elvis M., and yours can be Elvis D. Mine will be Elvis S."

I couldn't believe it. The other two Jennifers loved that idea.

"Isn't he cool?" Robin said as she traced her finger around the side of her snail's shell. "Maybe I'll call mine Curly."

"Hey, I know!" Marc said. "Why don't we call ours Larry and Moe? Like the Three Stooges."

I looked quickly at old Rotten Apple to see if she minded. She smiled and nodded. Too bad. We named them Larry and Moe anyway.

"Class, I want you all to see if you can get your snails to eat."

Marc made a face and a snoring sound. "Psst, Neil, wanna race them?"

"Sure."

We lined our snails up near the edge of the desk. Mine was Moe — he's my favourite Stooge. Larry was bigger and had dark brown stripes.

"The pencils will be the finish line," Marc said.

Without asking, Rotten Apple put Curly on the desk. Curly was beige and even bigger than Larry. He started creeping forward right away. Moe slimed around and went backwards. Larry

refused to budge, even though Marc nudged him forward a couple of times.

Curly surged past the pencils. "Whoa there, Curly! Good boy. Don't crawl off the desk."

Rotten Apple's snail *would* have to win the race! Too bad she scooped him up before he went over the edge.

"All right," Mrs. Leduc called. "It's time to go home. Put your snails back in their bottles. Be sure to stick the top parts back on with masking tape so they can't escape. Remember to take your book report forms home and bring your baseball mitts tomorrow. The weather's supposed to be sunny."

Chapter 5

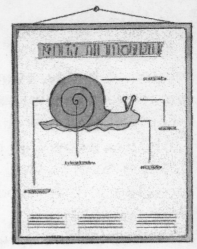

Snail Baseball

The weather report turned out to be right. Next morning, a big fried egg sun shone from a sky as blue as a swimming pool. No clouds anywhere. Would it stay like that till afternoon gym class?

"A snail's muscles produce waves which start at the front and move to the back, pulling it forward. Like a bulldozer."

I was only half-listening to Mrs. Leduc in between checking outside for signs of rain.

She pointed to a big snail poster. "They can move at about ten centimetres a minute. When they move slowly, it's called creeping. More quickly is called galloping."

Marc made horse noises and everyone laughed.

We put our snails away and did plurals for the rest of the morning. Finally, it was afternoon, and the weather was still perfect for baseball. I thought I would burst if we didn't go outside soon.

"All right, groups," Mrs. Leduc was saying, "when you're all finished doing your plurals, we'll go outside."

Everyone started working faster — you could tell by the loud scratching of pencils.

Marc, Robin and I were in the same group.

"Dog, dogs. Cat, cats. Mouse, mouses," Marc said out loud as he filled in his work sheet.

"Mice," Robin corrected, without looking up from her own sheet.

"Oh, yeah? Then how come houses aren't hice?" Marc snapped.

He had a point, I thought, as I chewed the end of my pencil.

"Well, more than one louse is lice," Robin told Marc.

I chewed my pencil some more. Rotten Apple was right as usual. And I hated it.

"Fox, foxes, ox, oxes," Marc kept going.

"Oxen, dummy," Robin told him.

"Robin, in grade three we do not call each other names!" Mrs. Leduc said as she walked by our desks.

Yay! Rotten Apple got in trouble for once.

"Marc, the plural of ox is oxen," Mrs. Leduc continued.

Rats. I'd put down oxes too. I tried to rub out my wrong answer but the eraser on the end of my pencil was wet from chewing. First the paper turned grey. Then the grey clumped into little worms. Then suddenly there was a hole where the s used to be.

Mrs. Leduc noticed. "Just write oxen neatly above the hole, Neil." She closed her eyes as she said it.

Phew! I thought she'd give me a new sheet, and make me start over.

"I'm looking for someone with their hand raised, who is finished their — " Mrs. Leduc started.

"Oh, oh! Pick me!" Marc interrupted.

"*And* who is sitting quietly," Mrs. Leduc continued. "Joshua, you may lead the class out."

Josh rushed out the door, down the hall and into the school yard. Everyone ran for the field.

"I'm up first!" I yelled, grabbing a bat and swishing it through the air.

"No, Neil. We'll continue where we left off yesterday. Except I want everyone on outfield to shift positions. Centre field to left, left to third base."

Mrs. Leduc rearranged the team. Then she checked her clipboard. "Andrew Constantine. You're up first."

Why did she have to pick today to start being fair? I wondered. I threw down the bat and headed for the end of the line.

Our team did okay for a while. Andrew even hit a homer, making the score 1–1. But then Tom stepped up to the plate.

He popped a fly past first. Robin stood there calmly, in exactly the right place, her glove in the air, ready. She pocketed the ball easily and tossed it back to Marc. I wanted to gag. Counting my pop fly from the day before, that made three out.

"This is snail baseball," I grumbled as I headed towards left field. At least now though, I could run and pick up balls instead of standing around.

I started to cheer up. "Come on, guys," I called out to my team. "We can do it!"

The game was going to get exciting. I could feel it.

Chapter 6

Accidentally on Purpose

The game got exciting, all right. But not the way I'd thought, and not for a while.

First, Zachary walked to first after about the millionth pitch. Then Becky and Kelly's hits barely trickled past the plate. Andrew took care of them all by himself. I ran back and forth just to keep awake.

Jennifer D. grounded a ball past first. Finally, something to do.

I moved in, remembering to put my body

behind the glove, just in case. But I trapped the ball, scooped it up and threw it carefully to first base. *Clup!* Craig caught it easily, long before Jennifer D.'s foot came close to the bag.

All right! We were up again.

Jenny took first base. Still three to go before my turn. I checked the sky. A couple of fluffy lamb-shaped clouds had strayed in to watch the game.

"Go, Craig, go!" I cheered as Craig made it to second.

"Get another run in, Christopher!" I called. Three more lamb clouds crowded together to watch him strike out.

"Come on, Rishad! Hit a homer!" Fat chance. Strike one, ho hum, strike two, strike three.

Finally, my turn.

By now, a whole flock of sheep clouds was sleeping in the sky above us. No danger they would rain us out.

I swung the bat through the air a couple of times. *Whoosh!* I felt the wind the bat made. Now Marc wound up and threw. I nicked the ball and it dropped at my feet.

"Foul one," Mrs. Leduc called.

The next pitch zoomed too close for me, so I stepped away and didn't swing.

"Strike two."

"What! Mrs. Leduc, that wasn't in the strike zone. Marc, tell her!"

"Neil."

"Yes, Mrs. Leduc?"

"Play ball."

"Yes, Mrs. Leduc."

Boy, did she make me mad. I imagined all the sheep clouds waking up to agree with me. "Ba-aa-aa-d call," they'd cry out together.

Over behind first base, I saw Robin standing on her hands as easily as if they were her feet. She grinned upside down. She thought I was an easy out.

"Oh, yeah, you stupid Rotten Apple? Just for that, I'm going to line drive the ball right past your nose," I yelled.

Marc gave me a thumbs-up sign. He pitched and I kept my eye on the ball. All my angry

feelings went into my swing. *Crack!* The ball turned into a bullet heading straight for Robin.

"Don't catch it, don't catch it," I said with each step that I ran. First base — I didn't dare look Robin's way, just in case. Second base, third base.

Nobody cheered as I dashed across home plate.

Maybe Robin had caught the ball after all. I kept my head down because I didn't want to know.

But no one cheered for her, either. Our class was never this quiet! Robin must have missed the ball for once in her life. I looked up.

Most of the class stood crowded in a circle behind first base.

"What happened?" I asked. But in a squishy place inside, I knew.

Marc walked back to join me. "Some line drive, Neil," he answered. "You hit Robin in the face."

"It got her nose," I heard Craig explain to someone beside him.

"I think it's broken," Zachary said, stepping away from the circle around Robin. Zachary looked as white as one of the lamb clouds.

"Ba-aaa-aaa-d!" the lambs seemed to bleat at me.

"It was an accident. I didn't mean to!" I explained to the backs of the kids around Robin. But even the clouds moved away and wouldn't listen.

Mrs. Leduc rushed Robin towards the school. Robin had her hands cupped around her face and blood was streaming through her fingers. But she wasn't crying.

So how come I wanted to?

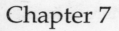

Chapter 7

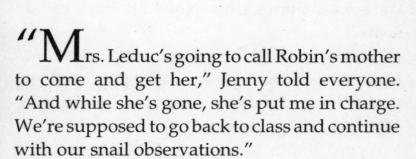

Disaster and More Disaster

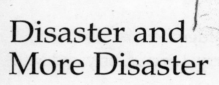

"**M**rs. Leduc's going to call Robin's mother to come and get her," Jenny told everyone. "And while she's gone, she's put me in charge. We're supposed to go back to class and continue with our snail observations."

"Come on, slugger, let's go," Marc said to me, slapping my back.

I ducked away from his hand but my feet didn't budge.

"Don't worry about Robin," Marc told me. "Nobody blames you."

I wished I could've talked to Robin to find out how she felt. To tell her I'd never hit that hard before in my life, and explain that I never dreamed the ball would bash into her face.

"What's wrong with you? Let's go." Marc pushed me.

I shrugged my shoulders.

"Come on. If we hurry, Larry, Curly and Moe can have a rematch."

Finally, I stumbled after Marc, through the school doors, down the hall, back to our seats.

"Hurry *up*, Neil. Mrs. L. will be back soon." Marc zipped the tape from the pop bottle so that we could lift out the snails. "Here, take Moe."

Would Robin have to go to the hospital? I stared at the snails till they became a blur.

Marc placed Moe in my hand. "Take Curly, too," he said and put him beside Moe.

"No, I can't. Curly belongs to Robin. We can't

just play around with him without her permission."

"Line them up, Neil."

Marc wasn't listening to me. I set Curly and Moe beside each other.

"Ready, set — " Marc squirted an eyedropper full of water onto Larry. "Go!"

I grabbed the tiny medicine bottle from Marc, refilled the dropper and squeezed some water onto Curly, too. It was the least I could do — take extra-special care of Robin's snail. The water seemed to energize Curly and he moved ahead. I squirted Moe, too but he just sat there.

Marc nudged Larry. Larry wouldn't budge. "Come on, giddyap, gallop!" he told him, nudging him harder. Then he lifted him up and moved him ahead a couple of centimetres.

Curly approached the pencil finish line.

"Turn him around!" Marc yelled at me. "Don't let him win. Larry's gaining on him."

At that moment, Mrs. Leduc walked into the classroom. "What is the meaning of all this noise?"

Marc and I looked up and away from the snails — just as Curly slimed over the edge of the desk. In a panic, I made a quick grab for him.

It was a quick, *hard* grab. I felt Curly's shell crack between my fingers.

"Oh, no!" First Robin's nose, now Curly's shell. Everything inside me sank down into my shoes.

Marc began explaining to Mrs. Leduc. "Sorry, we just noticed Larry eating some lettuce. I guess I got a little excited."

"All right. But please try to use your indoor voices while in the classroom. Especially when I'm out of the room."

"Yes, Mrs. Leduc."

Jenny Sommers raised her hand.

"Yes, Jenny?" Mrs. Leduc said.

"Is Robin okay?"

"I . . . I'm sure Robin will be fine," Mrs. Leduc answered. "Her mother's taking her to Emergency right now."

Emergency! Sirens screamed in my head. I

pictured Robin being wheeled on a stretcher down a hospital hall.

"Neil, what's wrong with you? You look like you're going to barf."

I pictured Curly lying on the stretcher next to Robin. I didn't want to open my hand to check on him and I couldn't answer Marc. Finally, I slowly straightened my fingers.

Marc snickered when he saw the small crack in Curly's shell.

I quickly covered Curly with my other hand. "It's not funny, Marc. How's Robin going to feel?"

"You're kidding, right? Rotten Apple? The girl you just beaned with the ball? You care about how she feels?"

"I keep telling you, I didn't do it on purpose."

"You said you were going to line drive it past her face."

"Yeah — past, not into, you moron!"

"Okay, okay. I don't know what you're getting so mad about."

"I'm not mad!" I snapped at him. I just feel

rotten, I thought to myself. As rotten as I used to think Robin was.

"Let me see Curly again. Maybe he's just a little hurt." Marc pushed my cover hand away. Curly looked as alive as a rock. "Maybe we should tape him up."

"No! We're going to put Curly back in the bottle and leave him alone."

"Fine by me. In he goes." Marc opened the bottle.

I gently placed Curly next to the greenest looking lettuce leaf. "Have something to eat, boy. You'll feel better."

But Curly didn't even peek out of his shell. We put Larry and Moe down next to him, hoping to encourage him out.

"What do you think, Marc? Is he going to be all right?"

Marc wrinkled his nose and twisted his mouth. "I don't know, Neil. But he sure doesn't look good."

Chapter 8

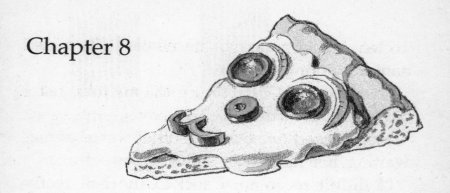

Tokens

"**W**hat's wrong with you, Neil?" Mom asked that night at supper as she touched my forehead. "You're not eating your pizza."

Two pepperoni eyeballs stared up at me. I peeled one off slowly and ate it. "Something happened at school today."

"Oh?" Mom put her slice of pizza down and looked at me.

"I . . . I hit someone."

"You were fighting?"

"No. It happened in baseball. I hit a girl named Robin Apple."

"Neil hit a girl, Neil hit a girl," my four-year-old sister Tara sang.

Mom closed one eye. The other stared at me, waiting, just like the last slice of pepperoni.

"I didn't mean to. I socked the ball really good. Only it plowed into Robin Apple's face."

Mom closed her second eye. Then she opened both eyes wide. "How is she?"

"I don't know. But her mother had to take her to Emergency."

Mom frowned as she stood up. "Well, I'll phone her parents right now and find out." Mom patted my shoulder. "Don't worry, Neil. It was an accident."

That's what I kept telling everybody. But was it really? Hadn't I wished Robin would fall on her face a million times? And hadn't I aimed the ball her way?

"Neil hit a girl," Tara repeated, grinning.

I turned to her. "Yeah, well you better shut up, or I might hit another one."

"Neil! That's enough," Mom snapped. "What's wrong with you?"

"I already told you. I broke a girl's nose!" I stomped off to my room. "And it was too my fault," I yelled as I slammed the door.

After a long while, Mom knocked.

I waited a few seconds. "Come in," I finally called to her.

"Neil, I spoke to Mrs. Apple. She says Robin has a small fracture. But it's not a bad one. She won't need an operation."

An operation? I punched the pillow on my bed. Now I pictured Robin being wheeled down a hospital hall. When the stretcher reached the operating room, a doctor with a mask on his face shook his head gravely.

What did a broken nose look like? How could Robin breathe with a cast on her nose? "Mom, can I go over and see her?"

"If it's all right with Mrs. Apple, certainly. And you can bring Robin a present." Mom squeezed my shoulder. "It might make you feel better."

"A present," I repeated. "But what could I give a girl?"

"Same thing you give a boy — something she likes. What does she enjoy?"

Hmm — books, dogs, baseball. What could I get? Then it came to me. "Hey, Mom, how about I give her some batting tokens for the cage at the Sport Palace?"

"That sounds good."

"Yeah, she'll love that. She's the best batter in the class."

"Better than you, Neil? I don't believe it."

I looked away from Mom and punched my pillow again. "Yeah, she's better than me, all right." I jumped off the bed. "Can we go right now?"

"Well, your father might be home any minute . . . "

"Come on, Mom. Dad's never on time."

My father is a police officer and he's always staying late to catch up on his paperwork.

"All right," Mom agreed. "I'll leave him a note. Just let me call Mrs. Apple first."

Mom came back from the phone with her car keys in hand. "Tara, put your sneakers on. We're going for a little ride."

At the Sport Palace, I used up the whole five dollars I'd saved from my allowance on the tokens. Three for Robin, two for me. With those tokens in my pocket, I felt ready to face anything. Maybe even Robin with a cast on her nose.

"Come in," Mrs. Apple said when she answered her front door. "Neil's here," she called.

Robin didn't answer.

Mrs. Apple smiled at me. "Why don't you go downstairs to the family room? She's resting on the couch."

I pulled three tokens from my pocket as I walked down the stairs. Following the sound of the TV, I found the family room. And Robin. She was lying on a couch with a book in her hand. The brown slimy worm hung between the open pages.

I was ready to face anything. Just not this.

Robin's eyes looked like they had sunk to the bottom of two purple holes. Her nose made me think of a balloon with knobs on it. One that's lost most of its air. She didn't have a cast on, though — not even a bandage.

"Hi," I said and waited for her to answer. She waved one finger.

"Nice bookworm," I said. "I gave mine to my sister. A boa constrictor for her Barbie, you know."

"Uh-huh."

Robin kept staring at the TV. Her eyes didn't seem to have laser power anymore. Or if they did, she didn't have them set on anything.

"Um . . . um, where's Prince? Your dog, I mean."

She looked at me for a second. Then her eyes dropped to the book. They didn't scan the page though. "My dad keeps Prince at his place."

"Oh, that's too bad."

I couldn't say anything else for a moment. Then I just had to ask. "Does it hurt much?"

Robin shook her head, then lifted her eyes. "It just looks gross." She faced me now.

"I think you look . . . awesome."

"Oh, sure. Bet you can't wait to tell Marc. So you can both have a good laugh."

"No, honest. Marc thinks black eyes are cool. He once drew one on with his mother's makeup."

From the bottom of those purple holes, Robin's eyes watched me.

"Well, here." I fingered the three tokens in my hand as I stretched out my arm to give them to her. They didn't seem enough. With my free hand, I dug out the other two and dumped all five into her open palm. "I brought you some batting tokens."

She looked at them and then up at me. For a moment I thought she might smile. "Why?" she asked.

"Because," I answered.

"Because why?" she asked again.

"Because I . . . I'm sorry."

Robin frowned and stared at the tokens again.

Was she going to throw them at me? No. Finally she closed her hand around them. "Thanks." She turned back towards the television.

Tara stomped down the stairs with Mom and Mrs. Apple following behind.

"Neil, Tara's getting restless," Mom said. "Are you ready to go?"

"Yeah. I guess."

"Mom," Robin said, holding up the coins, "Neil gave me some batting tokens for the Sport Palace. Do you think Dad can take me on Saturday?"

"It's not his weekend to have you, Robin. And Granny's coming, so I can't either."

"Aw, rats." Robin's mouth twisted down, making her face look even more sore.

"I can drive Robin and Neil on Saturday if you like," Mom suggested.

"That sounds good," Mrs. Apple agreed. "Don't you think so, Robin?"

Robin didn't look sure. "Yeah, that would be great, Mrs. Boisvert."

Then Mom started back up the stairs. I was

supposed to follow but there was one more thing I needed to tell Robin. "Robin," I started, "after you went to the hospital, we were supposed to observe our snails."

"Oh, yeah? How's Curly?" Robin smiled. "He sure is fast. For a snail, that is."

I looked at her face. Even with that balloon nose and those purple tunnels around her eyes, she looked happy and excited. I couldn't tell her about the cracked shell, not now. "He sure is," I said instead. "Too fast for his own good."

Chapter 9

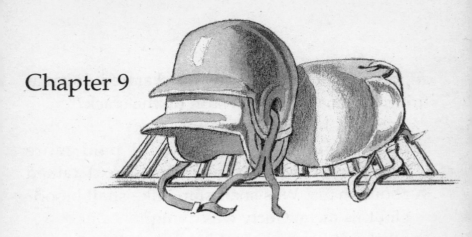

Zing, Clunk, Zing, Clunk

Friday morning, Robin's desk stayed empty. Her nose must hurt pretty bad, I thought. I rushed over to check on Curly but he wasn't there, either.

"Marc, Marc, I can't find Robin's snail."

"Take it easy. He's up at the top of the bottle."

"Is he okay?"

"I don't know. Let's check." Marc undid the pop bottle and shook it.

"Careful, Marc. We don't want any more breaks in his shell."

Curly fell out with a clunk. I stared down at him. "Ew, what's that stuff on the crack?"

"Slime, I guess," Marc answered.

For a moment, I wished I'd paid more attention to Mrs. Leduc when she'd talked about snails. Was snail slime like snail blood? Did this mean Curly was dying?

When Mrs. Leduc told us it was time for our plurals sheets, I also wished I'd paid more attention. Without Robin to help us, Marc and I had a terrible time.

"Bear, bears, moose, mooses," Marc read out loud as he filled in his sheet.

Jenny was in the group next to ours. She snorted and snickered. Robin never laughed at us like that.

"Hold on, Marc," I told him. "I think that could be meese. You know, sort of like goose, geese."

Marc chewed his lip and frowned. "It doesn't look right, Neil."

"Sure it does. Just keep going."

"Deer, deers . . ."

"No, I remember Mrs. Leduc calling us her deeries once . . . better put down deeries."

Marc frowned again. "Sheep. Um, would that be like ox — sheepen — or would it be sheepies?"

I stared at the words as I wrote them down. The truth is, none of them looked right to me.

Marc and I had so many wrong we ended up losing our recess. And then we did line dancing in gym that afternoon. It seemed even Mrs. Leduc didn't want to play baseball without Robin.

Next day was Saturday. Luckily, Dad was off duty for a change, so he minded Tara while Mom drove Robin and me to the Sport Palace.

"Hi, um, how's the nose?" I asked as she slid in the back seat beside me.

"Ugly," Robin answered, turning to face the window.

I couldn't talk to Robin with her not looking at me, so the ride was pretty quiet. She seemed happier as we ran through the parking lot and into the Sport Palace. We'd come early and the place looked empty.

The owner followed us to the back. A

teenager was batting in the pro ball cage. *Whomp, whomp* the ball went against the fence whenever he missed. FOR TWELVE YEARS AND OLDER, the sign said.

Robin shut her eyes with each whomp.

"You don't want to use that one," the owner told us. "The pitching machine in that cage throws the ball at over a hundred klicks an hour."

"Robin, do you want to go first?" Mom asked.

"No, thanks, Mrs. Boisvert," she answered quickly.

I turned to Robin and noticed she was squeezing her eyes shut each time the ball headed towards the fence.

"Don't worry, it can't come through the cage," I explained to her.

"I know that."

Zing. Robin squeezed her eyes shut. *Clank! Zing. Squeeze. Clank!*

"Your turn, Robin," I said when the teenager had finished.

Robin didn't move.

"You can go in the lob ball cage. It's a lot slower. That's where I go," I said when she kept staring at the pitching machine.

"That's okay, Neil. You go first."

"Um, I forgot to buy tokens. Mom . . ." I turned to ask her for a loan.

Robin tapped my shoulder. "Here, just take one of mine." She pushed it into my hand.

"Thanks."

I put on a helmet, grabbed a metal bat and stepped into the rookie cage. A red eye lit up on the machine when I pressed the start button. The ball flew out like a piece of popcorn. When the popcorn dropped, I missed. The ball clunked hard onto the floor. *Pop, clunk, pop, clunk.* I missed a few times.

"Eyes on the ball, Neil," Mom coached.

I looked away from the red eye and watched the ball. Pop. This time I connected. *Clank! Pop. Clank! Pop. Clank!* Nine pitches, then my turn was over.

"Okay, Robin."

Robin took a long time picking out a helmet

and bat. Then she walked slowly into the cage, raised her bat and stood there.

"Press the button!" I called to her.

She pressed it as though it might break.

"Harder!" I yelled when the red eye didn't light up.

She pressed again. The ball popped out of the machine and clunked onto the floor in front of her. She stepped forward. Her hands were twisting back and forth along the bat handle as though it were a jar she wanted to open.

The next ball popped out, and I saw her shoulders snap forward. But her bat didn't move. On the third ball, I noticed she closed her eyes. *Clunk.* The ball dropped to the floor again. Robin covered her face. *Clunk.* Four more pops, four more clunks. She never swung, not even once. Head down, Robin stepped out of the cage.

"It's okay. The first time I went in, I missed every pitch, too."

Robin looked at me, her eyes too shiny. "I come here all the time with my dad," she snapped.

My mouth dropped open. I didn't know what to say.

"Here, have these." She dumped the rest of the tokens into my hand then turned to Mom. "Mrs. Boisvert, I have a headache. Do you think you could take me home?"

"Of course. Neil, come on."

Robin walked quickly ahead of me and I noticed something else about her.

Her sneakers weren't lighting up anymore.

Chapter 10

Rattled Snails

The whole class grouped around Robin on Monday morning as she peered into our snail bottle. "Curly's hiding up near the cap and won't come down," she told Jennifer.

Robin's nose still looked like a knobby balloon, but it had turned a funny colour. Grey with streaks of beige. The tunnels around her eyes also looked chalked over with beige.

"What's that yucky dried stuff around your eyes?" Zachary asked, pointing at her face.

Marc snickered. "Rotten Apple's wearing makeup."

"Shut up!" I told him. "She's covering up the bruises."

Marc looked at her as though she were from another planet. "Why would you want to do that?"

"Because!" Robin grumbled.

"My cousin broke her nose and the doctor broke it again with a hammer," Jenny told Robin. "Is that what your doctor's going to do?"

Robin shook her head quickly. Everyone wanted to talk about Robin's nose except Robin.

"Grade three, that's enough snails for today. Back to your seats," Mrs. Leduc said. "We have a half-hour before the bell. The group that completes their plurals sheet first will be the first out for recess."

"Family, families, baby, babies, valley, vallies. . . " Marc read out.

"Valley just adds an *s*," Robin told him, looking over his shoulder. "You don't change the *y* to *ie*."

"Great. Thanks, Robin."

I'd spelled it with *ies* too. Boy, was I glad we had Robin back.

Then there were the bonus snail plurals. "Organ, organs, whorl, whorls, fungus . . . " Marc looked towards Robin.

"That's easy. You stick an apostrophe after the *s*. Just like for Santa Claus," she explained to him.

"An apostrophe!" I repeated. Recess was looking good.

"An apostrophe," Marc whispered as he wrote it down. He didn't show it, but I knew he was impressed.

We were going to get perfect on our sheet. Mrs. Leduc would let our group line up first — all thanks to Robin.

"Fungus becomes fungi," Mrs. Leduc said as she helped us correct our sheet a little later.

"Uh, Mrs. Leduc," Marc told her, raising his hand. "I think you have that wrong. I think we should just add an apostrophe after the *s*, like in Santa Claus."

"Very good, Marc," Mrs. Leduc answered. Marc grinned.

"But the apostrophe shows possession, as in Santa Claus' reindeer. Fungus does become fungi, just like octopus and octopi."

Marc turned in shock to stare at Robin. I did too. Robin wrong? She didn't even look back at us.

The recess bell rang then. Chairs scraped back loudly as everyone hustled to leave. "Class," Mrs. Leduc called over the noise, "Quietly, please."

"Mrs. Leduc, Mrs. Leduc," Jenny called, waving her hand in the air.

"Yes, Jenny, your group may line up first."

"But Mrs. Leduc, our bottle is open and the . . ." Jenny gulped, looked around, chewed her lip and gulped again. "The . . . Elvi have escaped."

Mrs. Leduc held up a hand. "All right. If we look together, we'll find them. Each of you, search the area around your desk for the Elvises." Mrs. Leduc hesitated. "Elvi," she corrected herself. "Snails," she corrected herself again.

We hunted fifteen minutes for the snails. No Elvis spottings anywhere.

"Maybe they went back to Graceland," Marc suggested.

The bell rang again.

"Aw, man, recess is over," I complained.

"Everyone, back to your desks," Mrs. Leduc ordered. "Don't worry, Jenny. We'll ask Mr. Kropp to keep an eye out for the Elvi when he cleans. I'm sure they'll turn up somewhere."

Everyone tiptoed around, afraid they might accidentally stomp on an Elvis. But I was afraid of something else.

Chapter 11

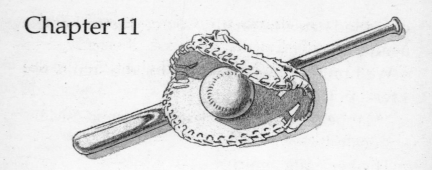

The Fat Lady Sings

That afternoon was perfect for baseball. Before we started to play, we decided to give our teams names.

"We want to be the Blue Jays," Josh called out.

"Why? You play like snails," Andrew muttered.

"That's it," Jennifer D. said. "The Mighty Snails."

So now my team was the Blue Jays, and Robin's was the Mighty Snails.

Robin was chewing on a fingernail as she slowly shuffled up to the plate. She picked up the bat and twisted her hands just like at the Sport Palace. She shifted her feet, frowned, and shifted them again. Finally, she wobbled the bat through the air a couple of times.

"Ready!" she said to Craig who was pitching for the Jays.

But she wasn't, I could tell. There was no laser beam in her eyes. From the bottom of those chalky grey tunnels, she stared blankly ahead. The pitch came, she twitched and missed. The second pitch came and she swung late. The third pitch whizzed by before she even began her swing.

The Mighty Snails were off to a bad start. Marc rubbed some dirt onto his hands and, as usual, pointed to where in his wildest dreams, some day, he might hit.

Our outfield all moved in.

"Tough luck, Marc!" I yelled when his bat whistled past the ball for the third time.

"Whooo hooo!" I cheered when Lindsay

struck out. "We're up, and it's my turn."

I stepped to the plate. Where was Robin? Playing second base. I wanted to make sure not to hit her again. First pitch, I tapped the ball gently towards third. Shock of shocks, Jennifer M. caught it.

"Can you believe it?" I complained to Andrew. "She picks now to start catching."

He shook his head and then stepped to the plate. "Come on. Home it! Home it!" I cheered.

Andrew cracked it over to left field. But this time, Jennifer D. snatched it up. Andrew stayed on second. Amazing! The Jennifers were playing the best game of their lives.

But the Blue Jays were playing better. Hurray! Tom, Shannon and even Selina batted great.

"Way to eye the ball," I yelled when Christopher passed up all Zachary's wild pitches and walked to first.

"Four–nothing, Blue Jays," Jenny called.

"Rishad, Rishad, he's our man," I started to cheer.

"If he can't do it, no one can!" the rest of the

Blue Jays joined in.

Rishad grinned, and popped a fly. The ball started sinking in the sky just ahead of Robin.

Too bad for you, Rishad, I thought.

I watched Robin move towards the ball as it curved downward. Forward four steps, back two, then forward two, glove raised to the sky. Yes, yes, Robin! The ball belonged to her.

And then she backed away, squeezing her eyes the way she had in the batting cage. The ball fell at her feet. She kept grabbing for it and dropping it like a hot potato.

"Aw, Robin! Come on," the Jennifers complained.

Christopher ran home and so did Rishad. The first home run of his life, I bet. And only the second time I could remember Robin missing a catch.

The Snails couldn't recover. Even the Jennifers fell apart. At 10–0, they finally stepped up to bat.

"It's not over till the fat lady sings!" I called to Marc, hoping to encourage Robin, too.

"The bell's going to ring in five minutes," Mrs. Leduc warned.

"Ten runs in five minutes is all you need!" This time I aimed my words straight at Robin.

Mrs. Leduc shook her head and waved everyone in. I stayed on second. She looked at me, opened her mouth, and started to sing. *"Tah, rah, rah, boom dee ay, we are all done today."*

"Aw, come on, Mrs. Leduc," I complained. "You're not even chubby."

Chapter 12

Dead Batteries

"Robin, Robin wait up!" I called when I saw her walking ahead of me after school. "How come your sneakers don't light up anymore?"

"The batteries died," she explained as she kept on walking. "My dad promised he'd bring me new ones soon."

"Hey, Robin!"

"What now?" She stopped for a second.

"Do you want to play ball with Marc and

me?" I didn't know what Marc would say about that but right then I didn't care.

"Very funny, Neil. I can't hit. I can't even catch."

"Everyone has a slump now and again."

"Oh, yeah!" Robin kicked a rock so hard it hit a stop sign. "Not like this, they don't." She frowned. "I'm afraid."

"You're afraid!" I repeated.

"Yeah. When the ball comes for me, I hear my nose crunch." She stared at her feet for a moment and then up at me. "You and your friend can have a good laugh."

I remembered her squeezing her eyes shut when the ball came for her. It made sense now. "We won't laugh at you, honest." But then I thought of Marc snickering at Robin's makeup and added, "I won't let him."

Robin started to walk away. "Come over to my house," I called. "I'll bat really soft balls. And I won't ask Marc to play till you get over it."

She stopped again. "Why would you want to help me?"

"Because."

"Because why?"

"Because I'm the one who broke your nose and made you afraid of the ball."

"Forget it. I was doing a handstand, remember? I should have been watching for the ball. So it was my own fault." Robin chewed at a fingernail.

"Come on. I really want to help."

"Oh, right." Robin kicked another stone. "You called me a rotten apple."

I thought for a moment. I'd hated Robin all this time only because she was good at stuff — baseball, spelling, you name it. And now I felt bad. "You're not rotten, okay?"

"Okay." Robin smiled. "I'll call my babysitter from your house."

When she'd finished talking on the phone, I grabbed my bat and glove and took her to the park across the road from our house. "I'll just bunt the ball a few times and you can take a few grounders."

Robin did all right with the grounders, so I decided to bat a pop. *Tok!* The ball sailed into the sky. Robin had plenty of time but she let it drop to the ground, then picked it up.

"Try catching it from the air now," I told her.

"I can't." Robin twisted her mouth around. "It might hit my face."

I thought for a few moments. "I have an idea that'll work for sure," I told Robin. "Come back to the house for a second."

I was so excited, I ran. Robin ran alongside me. "Mom, Mom!" I yelled the moment we stepped inside the door. "Can I borrow your old catcher's mask?"

"Sure. It's in the basement cupboard. Have some milk and cookies first."

I didn't want to stop, but Robin sat down and started talking to Tara. "What's your name? How old are you? Do you go to preschool?"

Marc would have gagged. "Cut it out, or she'll want to play," I warned Robin, but she didn't listen. Tara lifted up a bandage to show Robin her boo-boo, and Robin let her touch her nose.

"Can I play baseball with you?" Tara asked as we finished our snack.

"See!" I told Robin.

"Sure," Robin answered, shrugging her shoulders and smiling.

Tara grinned and then tore off to get her plastic bat and ball. I dug out Mom's catcher's mask, and we all headed back to the park.

"Give us five minutes, Tara. I'm trying to help Robin catch."

Tara nodded and sat on the bench to watch.

"Put this on, Robin. Then you don't have to be afraid for your nose."

Robin slid the catcher's mask over her face and positioned herself in the field.

Tok! Robin ran for my ball but misjudged where it was in the air. When the ball bounced along the ground, she fumbled for it.

I had been so sure this would work. I tried hitting it again, but she kept missing and picking up the grounders. Finally she flipped the mask up off her head. "It's no use, Neil. I can't see right with this thing on."

"Okay. Do you want to practise some more grounders? You can still be a great fielder if you pick up quick."

"You promised I could play." Tara stepped between us, holding her clown-sized bat and ball.

"Yeah, but I need to help Robin."

"Why?" Tara asked, sucking her finger.

"Because I'm afraid of the ball," Robin answered.

"Sing *Happy Birthday*," Tara mumbled around her finger.

"Can we just play ball here?" I asked impatiently.

"Wait a minute," Robin said. "What do you mean, Tara? It isn't my birthday today."

Tara giggled. "No, silly. You sing *Happy Birthday* so you won't be afraid."

"That is the dumbest — " I started to say.

"No, it's not," Tara interrupted. "Daddy told me to sing so I wouldn't be afraid of the dentist's drill. Only I had to sing inside my head because the dentist put his hand in my mouth."

I shook my head and rolled my eyes.

"Did it work?" Robin asked.

"Yup."

"Let her play," Robin told me. "Come on, Tara. Throw me the ball and I'll pitch for you."

Well, that made Tara happy all right.

Hollow and fat, her red bat gently popped the huge white ball into the air. Robin caught it. Robin pitched ten more times. Mostly Tara missed but when she hit, Robin caught the ball.

Then I pitched for Robin. *Slam!* The ball sounded different, more hollow, less sharp and hard. More like a *plop*. It's hard to be afraid of a *plop* noise.

Robin grinned. The lasers in her eyes seemed to switch on again and they were set on happy.

We played for another hour. A scrub game where we took turns pitching, fielding and hitting. That plastic ball never worked so hard.

"I helped Robin catch, I helped her," Tara said.

"You sure did," Robin told Tara. "Now if we could only play with a plastic ball and bat at school, I'd be all set."

Chapter 13

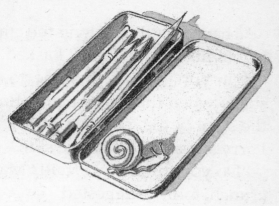

Galloping Again

"**I** cracked his shell when he went over the side of the desk. I guess I caught him too hard," I told Robin on Tuesday. "That's why he stays up near the cap all the time. I'm sorry."

She turned from the bottle and looked at me for a second. "I'm glad you caught him. He might have been hurt even worse."

Robin wasn't mad at me? I couldn't believe it.

"There was slime along the crack in his shell. Is that like snail blood?" I asked.

"Uh-huh. They use slime to close off their shells when they hibernate." Robin picked up the snail bottle, peering up at Curly. Moe and Larry stayed stuck on the side.

"Do you think he's afraid? Maybe he hears a crunch, too," I suggested.

"I think a snail's shell is like a fingernail. He'll get over it." Robin's eyes stared blankly from the end of those chalky grey tunnels. She didn't look sure.

I wasn't sure, either. About Robin. Would she ever get over her broken nose? After school, we always played with the plastic bat and ball. And in gym she still couldn't hit anything. When a ball came for her, she let it drop to the ground. I could almost hear her nose crunch, too, when I saw her eyes squeeze shut.

Tuesday, she'd struck out twice. Wednesday, she walked once and dropped every ball. Thursday, she struck out again.

Finally, it was Friday. The last day of baseball.

We had our spelling test, filled out another plurals sheet and were about to observe our snails. The usual stuff.

Then Jennifer M. screamed, "I found them, I found them! The Elvi, they're in my pencil box!"

The whole class gathered around her.

"How did they get in there?" Jennifer D. asked.

"I must have cleaned my desk without my glasses on and scooped them in." Jennifer M. scrunched up her nose and shrugged her shoulders. "They kind of look like my hockey puck erasers."

"So how come you didn't find them before now?" Andrew asked.

"It's my spare pencil box. The black pencil crayon was missing from my everyday case, so I checked in my spare box for one."

Marc rolled his eyes.

"Are they alive?" I asked. "They've been in there a long time."

Jennifer shrugged her shoulders and we all struggled to get a look.

"Oh, yuck! What are those little white round things sticking to the pencils?" Zachary asked.

Mrs. Leduc stepped in. "Better get the Elvi and their eggs into the bottle, Jennifer. One of them, or maybe all of them, are mothers."

Jenny squirted the Elvi with an eyedropper of water to revive them. They seemed okay.

"How many other people have eggs in their bottles?" Mrs. Leduc asked.

Tiny white balls turned up in eight more pop bottles. Since snails could be fathers and mothers at the same time, Mrs. Leduc said it would be impossible to tell exactly whose babies they were.

Marc sighed as he stared at our snails. "We don't have any eggs."

"Too bad," Robin said.

"Hey, look! Curly's moving. Curly's creeping! Yay, yay, Curly's okay!" I cheered.

"Let's get him out," Robin suggested.

We took out all three snails and lined them up on the desk. Larry and Moe started creeping but Curly did a perfect rock imitation.

Robin chewed at her thumbnail. Curly wasn't going to race. Then she bent over him, cupped her hand around her mouth and whispered something. Actually, it sounded more like singing.

Curly surged forward.

"I knew he'd get over it," Robin said proudly.

"He's galloping," I said.

"What a race horse," Marc growled. "He's beating Larry and Moe again."

Somehow, today, I didn't mind at all.

At lunch, we celebrated our growing snail families. It was pizza day anyway but Mrs. Leduc went out and bought donuts as well. When we finished eating, she told us that since it was our last baseball day and we'd been rained out a lot, we could play all afternoon.

"All right!" Neil shouted, reaching to slap my hand.

I slapped back weakly. "All right," I repeated softly. It could be all right, it could be great, if only Robin got over her fear of the ball.

It was my turn to be pitcher. Robin stepped to the plate. "Show me where you want it," I told her.

She wiped her hands on her shorts, turned her cap around backward and picked up the bat. Her hands twisted around the handle as she lifted her elbow. Then she swung a couple of times, straight and clean.

I pitched.

Robin didn't swing.

"Good eye, Robin!" Zachary shouted.

"Strike one," Mrs. Leduc called.

Zachary wrinkled his nose.

Robin took off her cap, slapped it against her hip, then set it frontward on her head. She swung at the air another couple of times.

"Pretend it's Tara's ball," I said quietly, but loud enough for her to hear. Then I pitched as soft and slow as I possibly could.

Robin hit the ball with a little *plop*, just outside the first base line.

"Foul ball, strike two!" Mrs Leduc said.

I pitched again and Robin plopped it to the same place.

"Move in closer!" Andrew told our outfielders. Then he stepped over to the base line, ready to catch Robin's next foul.

Robin took her hat off again and swept her hair back. Then she put the cap on backward. Her hands wrung the bottom of the bat.

"Come on, Robin, you're doing okay. Now slam it."

I saw her lips move as though she was mouthing some words. A light seemed to switch on suddenly in her eyes. Her laser beams were back! The ball headed for her. She didn't flinch or blink. She swung.

Chapter 14

Recharged Batteries

And what a hit! *Crunch!* The bat broke. The ball soared into the sky. It started coming down where the centre fielder would have been, if Andrew hadn't told him to move closer.

Robin ran. Her sneakers lit up! First base, second base, third — home.

"Yay, Robin!" I yelled. "Robin's got new batteries!"

Everyone crowded around her. Mrs. Leduc sent Zachary inside for another bat.

"Neil, why are you cheering for Rotten Apple?" Marc asked as we waited.

"She's not rotten."

"Says who?" Marc snapped.

"Says me. Do you want to play Frisbee with a real neat dog after school?" I asked him. We both looked over at Robin. She grinned.

"Okay, I guess," Marc said. "Since she's our slime partner anyway. You can cheer for Rotten — I mean Robin, if you want." He walked back to the head of the batting lineup.

Robin's home run didn't get the Snails galloping right away. Marc, Lindsay and Robby struck out super-quickly.

So then the Jays were up. I stepped to the plate. A couple of fluffy lamb clouds gathered above me. I wanted to swish them away. Robin stood just beyond second base, waiting and watching.

"Not over to centre field," I told myself. "Not over to centre field," I whispered to the ball as I knocked it gently to the side.

"Foul one, strike one," Jenny called.

"Aw, shut up," Marc told her.

Mrs. Leduc raised her eyebrow at him.

The next ball came too fast for me to think. Too fast for me to even try to aim it in some other direction. I smashed it hard. *Tok!* It headed straight for the lamb clouds.

"Ra-aa-aa-ad!" they seemed to bleat.

I started to run, keeping my head down, not daring to look. But then I had to. The ball started to drop just where it wasn't supposed to.

Everyone stared at Robin. If she caught it now, no one would mind about her missing the ball all the other times. If she caught it now, she'd be over her fear. If she caught it now, *I* could get over breaking her nose.

I saw Robin's lips move and thought I heard someone singing *Happy Birthday* ever so softly.

Slow motion, Robin backpedalled from centre field. Then she moved forward, her glove high in the air. But it was shaking.

She lowered her arm. She was going to shut her eyes, I knew it.

"Louder," I yelled at her. Robin looked my

way. "So you can't hear the crunch!" I started singing, "*Happy birthday to you, happy birthday to you.*"

Everyone stared at me, but I didn't care. Robin smiled. The lasers in her eyes clicked on, and her mitt rose.

Clup! I love the sound of a softball hitting a glove. It's smooth and soft and makes you feel powerful. Especially when the ball's in *your* glove. Or your friend's.

"Yay, Robin!" I cheered, and did a perfect cartwheel. The rest of the season was going to be great.

I love baseball.

Author **Sylvia McNicoll** has written several popular books for children, including *Bringing Up Beauty*, *More than Money*, *Blueberries and Whipped Cream* and *Project Disaster*, another story about Neil Boisvert. She lives in Burlington, Ontario with her husband and three children.